It Happened in Riverdale

It Happened in Riverdale, Volume 1

Juliana Harvard

Published by Juliana Harvard, 2021.

This is a work of fiction. Similarities to real people, places, or events are entirely coincidental.

IT HAPPENED IN RIVERDALE

First edition. May 19, 2021.

Copyright © 2021 Juliana Harvard.

ISBN: 979-8201913724

Written by Juliana Harvard.

Table of Contents

To Sandra Lee Miller who encouraged me to write about
growing up in Riverdale

It Happened in Riverdale

Riverdale is a fictional place in the 1960s. These stories reflect the flavor of that time, as heard through the voice of teenager Julie Scott. Although the stories are sometimes maudlin and melodramatic, sexist and gender stereotyped, filled with all the idioms and clichés and rhetoric stereotypical of a conservative small-town Christian community of that era in southern California, they represent intense expressions of a forgotten reality.

Juliana Harvard wrote the stories in an era when the word "gay" meant "happy" or "joyful" and nothing more. The word for homosexual was "queer." Funny how history has a way of repeating itself!

Book 1

THIS "TITLE STORY" is set in a fictional time of November-December 1959 and serves to introduce the main character Julie Scott and many other characters through their relationship dynamics and activities with the Riverdale Youth Club. The RYC sponsors a weekend campout at Pine Cove, a mountain retreat, just before Christmas. The Epilogue of this mini-novella, however, skips ahead to a projected time of several years into the future to a wedding day—the 1960s' "ideal" culmination for any young woman's adulthood—this one for Julie's best friend, Sandra Lee.

Chapter 1. The Big Four

IT WAS A COLD, DARK night in late November. Few stars shone in the moonless sky and an eerie wind played a haunting tune in the bare treetops. Steve Emory lay fast asleep in his room. He had strewn his clothes around the room and had not pushed the top drawer of his dresser all the way in. He had left one window halfway up, and the breeze played tag with the curtain.

When the clock struck twelve, this same breeze carried the sound of the midnight chimes from the big clock in the courtyard to Steve's ears. He turned over restlessly, gave one kick, and opened his eyes. Then he knew he had only been dreaming. He had been running from two monsters, Culture and Society. But as he ran, they had called after him, "Rebel! Rebel!" And he became only more entangled in their traps.

"Boy, what an imagination my subconscious mind must have," he thought as he turned over. But the more he tried to sleep, the more he thought about his crazy nightmare. Finally, from sheer exhaustion, he dropped off to sleep.

When morning came, Steve had quite forgotten the experience of the night before. He dressed and ate and started for school, as usual, his old gay self. Little did he know today would be the beginning of a turning point in his life. He arrived at school at the usual time, 8:00, and saw the same familiar faces. He had taken his books to his locker and was on his way to history class when he felt a soft hand touch his shoulder. He turned to see Cynthia's smiling face.

"Good morning, Steve," she greeted. "Did you just get here?"

Steve grinned and nodded and automatically took hold of her soft, tiny hand.

"Well," she said, "I guess you haven't seen the announcements on the bulletin board."

He shook his head and walked over to the bulletin board where someone had placed a large colored poster. After reading it silently, he turned back to Cynthia. "So," he said, "the first formal banquet of the year, huh?"

Cynthia nodded, her eyes shining. "And Ella—she's on the social committee, you know—says it's really going to be spectacular this year."

Steve knew right well what Cynthia, his girl for the past two years, was expecting now—an invitation. But just then the bell rang, and Steve said, "See you—got to run now"—and he ran.

Meanwhile, in the chemistry classroom, Julie had been going over her lesson before the bell rang. Suddenly Sandra burst into the room, her face beaming. "Look, Julie, look, will you? It's happened, finally! I told you Ken and Ella would never last. Just read this, Julie, just read this!" She held out a small, wrinkled piece of paper. Julie took the note and read it. A knowing smile crossed her face.

"What's the matter? Don't you think it's pretty neat?" asked Sandra.

"Yeah, sure," said Julie, trying her best to act normal. "Ah, read it out loud to me."

"'Dearest Sandra,'" she began, "'Ella and I are split up for good. But I've been thinking about you for a long time. I'd like to take you to the banquet, doll. Let me know as soon as you can. With all my love, Ken.' Oh, Julie, isn't it wonderful?"

"Yeah, sure," said Julie, "wonderful."

When Julie and Sandra went to the cafeteria for lunch that noon, Ken, Steve, Cynthia, and Ella were at their usual place. They seemed as happy and gay as ever. The "Big Four," as some kids called them, didn't look as though anything had happened or was going to happen that would ever break them up.

Sandra turned confusedly to Julie. "I don't get it. Look at 'em."

"I know, but they won't be like that for long," Julie said.

"How do you know?"

"Instinct," replied Julie.

Sandra said no more but was growing suspicious. In a matter of a few hours, she confirmed her suspicions. She had asked Julie to stop at the Snack Shop for a malt on the way home, but Julie had a music lesson. So Sandra went there with Carolyn instead. They sat down in the booth next to the one where the "Big Four" sat.

"All right, Ella," Ken was saying. "You'd better start talking."

"No, no," Ella giggled. "Leave me alone."

"You wrote that note, didn't you, didn't you?"

"Okay, okay," she screeched, "let me go and I'll tell you."

Ken relaxed his grip on her shoulders. "Okay, start talking."

"We only did it because—"

"We?" Ken interrupted. "Who's 'we'?"

"Julie and I," Ella continued. "We just wanted to get your reactions, and Sandra's."

"You little—" Ken shook his fist in mock anger at her. "It would serve you right if I went to the banquet with Sandra."

Ella only laughed, but Ken was getting serious. Anyway, Sandra had heard all she wanted to, so she got up and left.

"I wouldn't laugh if I were you," warned Steve. "Ken might just show you."

"I don't care," said Ella, tossing her head carelessly.

"You don't think I would, do you?" Ken said.

Until this time, Cynthia had been looking on with an amused smile. She broke in with, "Oh, say, Ella, Jim wanted your phone number last night—"

"Jim who?" broke in Ken, who spoke with a slightly worried tone.

"Her brother, who do you think?" replied Ella. Then turning to Cynthia, she said, "Go on."

"Well," continued Cynthia, "it seems he asked Sandra to go to the banquet with him and she refused, so he thought about you and—"

"And so he wanted my phone number, huh?" finished Ella. "Did you give it to him?"

"I thought I'd better check with you first," replied Cynthia.

Ella nodded her approval. At that moment, a girl rushed up to the table. Cynthia recognized her as the associate editor of the school paper. She had been over to Cynthia's house several times to work with her brother Jim, who was editor-in-chief of the paper. "Excuse me," the girl said, "but have any of you seen Sandra Lee? I was across the street and I saw her come in here. I've got some really exciting news to tell her."

The kids shook their heads. "We haven't seen her, JoAnn," said Cynthia. "I could give you her telephone number and maybe you could call her if the news is very important."

"Thanks," JoAnn said, "but I don't have a phone." She sighed. "I guess I'll just have to wait until tomorrow to tell her that Jim asked me to the banquet. Well, sorry to disturb you." And she started away.

"Wait a minute," Ken called to her. "Don't mind me being snoopy, but Jim who?"

"Why, Jim Donaldson," answered JoAnn, slightly startled. "You know, Cynthia's brother."

At that point, Ella coughed, Cynthia turned red and covered her face with her hands, Ken turned a deep purple, Steve burst out laughing, and JoAnn shrugged her shoulders and walked away. After a moment of very uncomfortable silence, Ken said to Cynthia, "Maybe that girl JoAnn doesn't have a phone, but I do. Do you, ah, have Sandra's number handy?"

"Oh, now, look, you two!" Steve interrupted. "I think this little game has gone far enough. You're not really going to bust us up, are you?"

"Right now, I'm not sure," snapped Ken. "Anyway, you don't have any room to talk, you know."

"Well, at least I didn't fuss—" He stopped short and covered his mouth.

"What do you mean?" asked Cynthia. "You didn't fuss with who?"

"It isn't anything, probably," reassured Ella. "Forget it."

"Hey, look at the time," said Steve, changing his tone. "We'd better be getting on home. Remember, I'm treating you guys today." He reached into his pocket for some change to pay for the sodas. As he did, a shiny metal object fell to the floor. He dived for it and tried to stuff it back into his pocket before anyone saw what it was. But he was too late. Cynthia had it in her hand.

"My ring!" she exclaimed.

"Correction," said Ken. "Steve's ring."

"Yes, but he gave it to me 'cause we're...going...steady..." Her voice trailed off, and she eyed the other three suspiciously. They looked at one another, none of them daring to speak a word.

"Now I'm putting it all together," Cynthia continued. "No wonder you didn't ask me to the banquet the minute you saw the announcement. I knew I had put your ring on the bench by the jukebox that day at the pool when we had our swimming party. I thought I had lost it, and all the time you had it!" She shifted her gaze toward Ken and Ella. "And you two knew it all the time. Of course, you'd know, Ken. But, Ella, why didn't you tell me that Steve had somebody new—"

"Honest, Cynthia," Steve interrupted. "It's not somebody new. I—I just, well, want to 'play the field' awhile."

"But don't you realize what you're doing to us?" Cynthia persisted. "The four of us, I mean?"

"But we can still be friends," Ken argued.

"That's not the point!" Cynthia snapped back. "You just don't understand! Anyway, when you knew about it, you shouldn't have kept it from me so long!" Then, turning toward Steve, she softened her tone. "All right, if that's the way you feel, okay. Be a wolf and have your fun. Forget I even exist. Forget all those good times we had together. Forget that graduation night two years ago and all the promises you made. Forget it all!" She paused. "But, Steve, I won't forget, I can't forget. And someday you're going to be tortured and hurt by somebody. Remember what I said, Steve Emory, someday you'll be sorry!" With that she got up and left, still clutching the ring in her fingers. Steve started after her, but Ken shook his head.

"Let her go," he said. Steve shrugged and sat back down. He started to say something and then stopped. For a few minutes, everyone was silent. Finally, Steve could bear it no longer, so he excused himself with, "See you kids tomorrow."

"Steve?" Ella called to him.

"Yes?" he said without turning around. Ella made no reply. Steve whirled around. "Aw, look," he said, "I'm just as sorry as you are that it had to happen like this. But it was going to come out sometime anyway, so," and he shrugged, "this is the way it happened. I didn't want to hurt her, but she knew as well as I did it wouldn't last for eternity. She should be able to accept some facts."

"You always told her it would last for eter—"

"Aw, Ella," Steve said disgustedly. "You're as naïve as she is. For pity's sake, every fellow has a line of some sort."

Ella rose to her feet, shaking her head slowly. "You men are all alike," she said as she departed.

"Aw, forget it," Ken told him. "Let's go."

Chapter 2. Banquet Night

IN THE DAYS THAT FOLLOWED, none of the kids at school seemed to detect the uneasiness within the "Big Four." Then came the night of the banquet. Ella and Cynthia went "stag." Ken, as Ella had suspected, took Sandra. Steve, much to everyone's surprise, took Carolyn Bullenhacker, who was notoriously known as the "little wolverine."

"I told you," Cynthia whispered to Ella, "that Steve was quitting me for another girl."

"Oh, Cynthia," Ella said, "I wouldn't pay any attention to it if I were you. You know Carolyn's reputation. Steve was probably trapped into asking her tonight."

Cynthia only shook her head and refused to listen.

"Listen, honey," Ella advised her, "no man is worth that much. Forget him. He's not the only star in the sky."

"I can't forget him!" Cynthia wailed. "I have always loved him, and I always will!" And she ran into the powder room. Ella shook her head in pity.

Meanwhile, Ken and Sandra were playing a pretty big game of pretending. To the onlooker, they were enjoying themselves to the fullest. But Ken was concentrating on Ella, doing everything he could to make her jealous. And although it seemed pretty exciting to Sandra to be having a date with Ken—her very first date—she was secretly drooling over Jim Donaldson, her childhood sweetheart from sixth grade. She had first gotten a crush on him at a party when they were playing Spin the Bottle and he had given her a peck on the cheek. For Jim, the infatuation had lasted only a few weeks, but on Sandra's part it still lasted, and her admiration had deepened. Now Jim Donaldson was having a good time with JoAnn and was totally unsuspecting of his secret admirer.

Just then Sandra's thoughts were interrupted. "Sandra, look over there," Ken was saying. "Do you see what I see?" He chuckled softly.

Sandra looked in the direction Ken was looking and saw what Ken was laughing at. Poor Julie had a problem. As the first banquet of the year for Riverdale High was for the junior high too, the place was swarming with seventh and eighth graders. And three of them surrounded Julie.

Two seventh-grade boys, Billy and Dennis, and an eighth grader, Eddy, had been secretly fighting over Julie. Now they were bringing the battle out into the open. They had all three endeavored to escort her to the table, all three had tried to sit by her, and now they were "discussing" who was going to "take" her home. And they were doing it in no uncertain terms. Julie's embarrassment was written all over her face. After a long struggle, Eddy dropped from the race. Then Dennis came up with a bright suggestion.

"Wait a minute," he said. "Why are we fighting like this? I think Julie should have something to say. It's a lady's privilege to go with whoever she wants to."

"That's right," agreed Billy. "Well, Julie, is it going to be me or him?"

Quite taken by this sudden announcement, Julie did not know just what to say. Hoping to stall for time to figure things out, she said, "Well, since you fellows have to be so formal, I will not cast a vote until I have heard a 'campaign speech' from both of you."

So while they were throwing their line at her and making ridiculous promises, Julie thought. She could tell they meant business in their own small way, and she couldn't just drop it. Why and how had this all started in the first place? Seventh-grade boys don't fight over freshman girls every day. Well, she was little for her age and a year younger than she was supposed to be for her grade because she had started school in another state when she was five years old. And her dimpled baby face didn't help matters much. But still—seventh graders? That was exaggerating a little too much.

She glanced at Eddy, who was still looking on with amused concern. He was her age, even though he was an eighth grader. She looked back at the other two. Billy was a little doll, and Dennis was the "brainchild." They were both pretty popular. She looked back at Eddy. He was a combination of them both. Oh, if only she were a couple years younger, she'd have it made.

"Aw, don't listen to him," Billy was saying. "He'll never keep any promises."

"He's the one who never keeps any promises," Dennis insisted, "You know he's just a wolf, anyway."

"Oh, yeah?" Billy retorted. "Well, you're just a gopher," he said, knowing Dennis was sensitive about his slightly protruding front teeth.

Julie, recognizing the purpose of the remark, scolded, "Now that's enough, both of you! Now tell me, Billy, what would your reaction be if I chose Dennis?"

"W-why, I guess I wouldn't like it very well," he stammered.

"But would I still be your friend?"

"Any friend of Dennis is no friend of mine," he bluntly replied.

"What about you, Dennis," Julie asked, "if I should choose Billy?"

"Well, I don't suppose I'd like it very well either," Dennis said, "but I wouldn't hate you for the rest of my life if you did."

"What would you do?"

"What could I do," he said, "but go back to the girls in my class."

"Without a fight?" Billy asked rather roughly.

"It wouldn't do me any good," said Dennis.

"Oh, brother!" muttered Eddy, who had been silent until now.

Julie looked at him and smiled as if reading his mind. Then she turned back to the other two and said with a most sober face, "Just as I thought. Both of you show too many signs of immaturity to have a girlfriend."

This statement startled Billy and Dennis. But Julie was not finished. "This may come as a shock to you but, Billy, I am not a soft little thing who swallows flattery and a big line. Neither am I a hard-headed woman, Dennis, who won't listen to reason."

"You see, fellows," said Eddy, not boasting, "you just don't understand women."

"Now just a minute, big brother," said Billy, "who gave you a right to butt in?"

"This is a free country, isn't it?" Julie stuck up for him.

"Yeah, but he said—"

"Never mind what he said," argued Julie. "I've decided."

"E-Eddy?" asked Dennis, wrinkling his nose.

"Eddy," Julie answered emphatically.

"Boy, what a sneaky thing to do!" Billy mumbled under his breath.

Paying no heed to him, she turned to Eddy, saying, "It's getting sort of late. Don't you think we'd better start home?"

Eddy smiled. "Better luck next time, fellows," he said. Then nodding to Julie, he said, "Okay, let's go."

Since Julie's house was just three blocks east of the school and Eddy's house was one block north of hers, it did not take them very long to walk the distance. Most of the way they walked in silence, both of them too timid to talk. It was a beautiful night, however, with the full moon shining high above the treetops and casting a strange glow on the red, yellow, and brown leaves on the ground.

"How did you know the way I felt about you tonight?" Eddy said to break the silence.

"Well," she said, "fellows who really like a girl enough won't do anything to embarrass her in public like Billy and Dennis were doing."

"Yes, but I could have meant what I said when I said I would surrender and let the other two divide you."

"Well," she smiled, "I kind of had a feeling you didn't."

By this time they were on Julie's front porch. Eddy didn't know what else to say then but, "You're sweet." And he lifted her head gently with his hand. "I only wish we were a couple years older," he whispered. But she pulled away.

"I think I see a light in the kitchen," she said. Touching his hand slightly, she whispered, "Thanks for everything. I'll see you."

There was a moment of silence as her pretty brown eyes gazed into his radiant face. It was as if they were communicating with some strange radar with a mutual message of, "I like you, too." Then she turned and disappeared into the house.

Chapter 3. In the Park

THE NEXT DAY, AROUND two o'clock, two girls were walking in the park. They wandered to a secluded, shady spot hidden among the trees.

"So you think he really likes you for his girl, huh?" Julie asked.

"Why else would he act the way he did last night?" Sandra asked.

"Sandra, I've got to tell you something," Julie said. "Ken didn't write that note. Ella and I did."

"I know," Sandra calmly replied. Seeing Julie's startled expression, she added, "Ken told me last night that you and Ella forged it."

"You're not mad at me for it, are you?" asked Julie.

"Mad at you!" Sandra exclaimed. "Mad at you because I got a date with Ken out of it? Or mad at you because he likes me now instead of Ella?"

"Well," laughed Julie, "I'm happy for you, but don't trust Ken too much."

"What do you mean?" asked Sandra in surprise.

"You just can't trust men too far," Julie answered.

"Well, Ken's different," answered Sandra. "You don't know him. He's just wonderful, Julie. You've probably never had a boyfriend like him."

Well, Sandra was right. Julie had never had a boyfriend like Ken. Every boyfriend she ever had was about her age or younger. She had never had one older than she was. Except for Dick. He was five months, fourteen days, and seven hours older. They would still probably be going together if he hadn't moved away. They had lived next door to each other for as long as she could remember. They had grown up together. Then, in the summer of seventh grade, his dad was transferred a thousand miles away. No one knew the childish agony Julie had gone through trying to forget him. Not that she was so madly in love with him, but every place she went and everything she did brought back memories of days that she could never relive.

"Well," said Julie now, "good luck with Ken."

Sandra sighed and leaned back on the grass. After a moment, she sat up and said, "Oh, Julie, how did things go for you last night? I noticed Billy Kingston and Dennis Holman were giving you a pretty rough time."

Julie smiled, then related the details.

On the far side of the park, two boys were having a conversation, discussing women.

"Aw, Steve," Ken was saying, "you don't need to quit Cynthia just because I'm going with Sandra now."

"I'm not, honest," answered Steve. "I had been thinking about it for a long time before that."

"You didn't say anything about it until I got mad at Ella."

"Well, that's just the way it happened. I didn't drop my ring in the Snack Shop on purpose."

"I still think you should apologize to her. She's a real sweet girl."

"What about you make up with Ella?"

"Oh, look," Ken said, as he nervously whittled at a twig with his pocketknife, "it's not the same thing. Ella's just too independent. She's too sophisticated, too. I'm just not her type. I want a woman to be soft and tender and weak."

"And I take it Sandra's that kind of girl?"

Ken sighed. "At first, I only asked Sandra to the banquet because I wanted to show Ella she wasn't the boss. And I wanted to make her jealous. But, I'm telling you, she has the hardest head this side of the Mississippi. I just gave up on her. Now Sandra's more my kind of girl." And he sighed again. "Now I've given you my reasons," he continued, "and they're all perfectly good ones. Now suppose you give me your reasons for quitting Cynthia. I couldn't think of one good reason you should stop going with such a cute girl as Cynthia."

"Well," said Steve, "she may be cute, but that's not all that counts, you know. She's cute, yes, but the trouble is she knows it. And she thinks she owns me. You may think that Cynthia never talked back and stood up to me the way Ella did to you, but Cynthia had her own secret way of getting me to do whatever she wanted me to. I was just getting a little tired of it. Anyway, a guy can have a lot more fun if he isn't going steady with just one girl."

Ken got up and stretched. "Let's go get a Coke or something, cat," he said. "But just wait until spring comes. You'll go right back to her or to some girl. You can't go without going steady for long. I know you!"

Steve said nothing but shook his head and thought, "I'll show you how wrong you are, Ken, old man. Wait until spring comes. Just wait." And he followed him to the hot dog stand.

Chapter 4. Trip to Pine Cove

IN THE WEEKS THAT FOLLOWED, Ella and Cynthia weren't very happy about what had happened between them and the boys. However, Cynthia showed it more than Ella did. Steve had been going with Carolyn lately, mostly because Cynthia would have been hot on his trail if he didn't appear to have a girlfriend. Cynthia knew enough to know that meant "hands off."

On the weekend that started Christmas vacation, the Riverdale Youth Club sponsored an outing. It was to be a weekend in the mountains at the Riverdale Youth Camp, which was located a half mile north of Pine Cove Village on Pine Cove Hill, about 24 miles east of Riverdale.

The snow had been falling every night since Wednesday, and on Friday morning it was about two feet deep. Ken took Sandra, Steve and Carolyn, and Julie and Eddy with him in his dad's car. It took them about 40 minutes to arrive at the RYC Camp. After they had located their cabins, they all met back at the lodge and took a walk in the new-fallen snow.

It was a perfectly beautiful day in the mountains. Around the lodge, the tall stately pines stood out like pretty candles on a frosted birthday cake. The swimming pool, so actively in use during the summer months, was now drained and covered. Here and there a gray squirrel chattered saucily and scampered up a nearby tree. Across the wooden bridge that spanned the frozen creek almost right for ice skating, the pathway led through Hickman's Forest. Here, as far as the eye could see, over hill and dale, the snow lay like a frosty carpet.

As the six of them wandered among the trees, some without leaves and some evergreen, they came upon a pond where the icicles dangled their stiff fingers in weird patterns. Here they each plucked a natural "popsicle" to suck on. Beyond a nearby hill, they could see the top of an old, deserted cabin. The snow lay on the roof like a blanket and icicles hung over the edge like the fringe of a giant bedspread.

Before returning to the camp, the teenagers hiked to the top of the highest hill called Pintail Peak. From here they could view the entire valley. The air was chilly and crisp, and their cheeks were turning rosy from the walk up the hill. There were a few silent moments as the group stood on top of the hill and viewed the scene below. When one is alone or with a loved one in a time and place like his, one is filled with a new awe and reverence for the Creator of this magnificent beauty.

All too soon they had to start back to the camp for the Campfire Program at sundown. In the winter, the program was held around the big open fireplace in the lodge. Ever since Ken had broken up with Ella, Eddy had become quite fascinated with Ken's new "heart throb" as he called it. And ever since he had started going with Julie, he had not been so quiet and conservative as before. Ken, who was a wolf, had become Eddy's teenage idol. Everything Ken did, Eddy tried to copy.

On his way to the lodge from the cabins earlier in the day, Eddy thought he heard Ken say something "suggestive" about Sandra to Steve, and he had exaggerated upon it in his own mind. Now, as they sat watching a moving picture, Eddy thought he had to do everything Ken did. And he was getting a little too fresh with Julie for his own good.

When the picture was over, some kids took a moonlight stroll before turning in. The full moon, new-fallen snow, and young lovers made quite a combination. Pine Cove Village was close to the camp, and before long they had wandered into Pine Cove. So why not have a hot chocolate or something before starting back out into the freezing winter night?

After a half-hour at the Pine Cove Sundae Shoppe, the kids decided that had better start back. Or before they knew it their moonlight stroll would turn into a midnight stroll. On the return trip, the couples walked four abreast along the deserted road. Some fellows, like Ken, thought it necessary to help keep the girls warm. Sandra and Julie were not ordinarily the girls who let boys put their arms around them every day. But tonight was an exceptionally frosty night.

Sandra and Ken and Eddy and Julie were walking together, the girls on the outside, when Eddy started whispering to Ken. "Why don't you kiss her?" it sounded like to Sandra. Julie thought he said, "I'll kiss Julie if you'll kiss Sandra."

When they reached the outskirts of the camp, lights were on in only two cabins. One was that of the camp director and his wife; the other was the cabin of Ella and Cynthia. All the others had either turned in early or had gone on the moonlight walk. There was a twelve o'clock curfew, and now the young people had exactly 13 minutes to midnight, at which time the camp director checked each cabin to make sure the lights were out and the occupants were sleeping. If anyone was missing, the Pine Cove police were ready to aid. However, Mr. Marcos, the Camp Director for the past three years, usually gave five or ten minutes' grace. But if you were careless and stayed out too long, he could cause a raucous.

When Eddy and Julie and Sandra and Ken came to the gate of the camp, they paused for a moment under the star-filled sky and let the others go on ahead. Sandra and Julie looked at each other, wondering what the boys had up their sleeves now. Ken looked at Sandra as if to say, "This wasn't my idea; it's all Eddy's planning." Just then Eddy broke the silence.

"Well," he said, giving Julie a wolfish look and then glancing toward Ken, "how about it? It's nice and dark over behind the craft building."

"Eddy!" Julie spoke in a tone of reproof and broke away from him.

"Aw, doll," he tried to argue, "just this once. They won't see us. Nobody will ever know."

"Listen, Eddy, you're a real swell kid. I like you a lot; at least, I thought I did. But there is a limit. If you want to make out, that's your business, but not with me. As much as I like you, I mean what I say."

"Aw, baby, please," he pleaded, "just one itsy-bitsy, teeny-weeny little kiss."

"No!" persisted Julie. "N-O, no!"

But Eddy refused to take a hint. "But you've done it before," he kept on. "I've heard all about that graduation night."

At that remark, a strange look came into Julie's eyes. "Please, let's not talk about graduation night," she said, her voice sounding as if she were almost ready to cry. With that, she turned and ran toward her cabin.

Bewildered, Eddy looked helplessly at Ken for a second. Then he ran after Julie. But she had slammed the door and locked it before he could reach her. Giving Ken and Sandra one last glance, Eddy slowly started toward his own cabin.

Now, in the starlight, Ken gazed at Sandra's lovely face. "Sandra," he began softly, "there's something I want you to know. When I first started dating you, my sole purpose was to just make Ella jealous. But she started getting too high-toned, thought she was just too good for me. Anyway, I've found out she isn't my type. Maybe you didn't know it, but Ella and I had only been going together for about four months, not nearly as long as Steve and Cynthia had been together. Since Ella is her best friend and Steve is mine, we four always palled around together. But," he paused, "let's talk about 'us.'"

Sandra smiled, half in amusement and half in contentment. When she said nothing, Ken went on.

"Since I've been going with you," he said, "I've discovered you're the girl of my dreams. Tell me," and he winked, "where have you been all my life?"

Sandra only smiled and blushed. There was a moment of uncomfortable silence on Sandra's part, for she was very ill at ease, not knowing what to say or do. For Ken, it was a moment of decision. He sighed then said, "Sandra, all those things I said to you the night of the banquet and every Saturday night since then, well, most of the stuff was just mechanical, but—but, Sandra, what I'm saying to you tonight, I really mean it."

She looked up into his face. He was serious. She could tell by his expression. He had never been like this before. His deep blue eyes seemed to tell her that he, Ken Nelson, belonged to her if she would only take him.

"Sandra," he said, "will you...will you go steady with me?"

Sandra was speechless. "I—I don't know," she stammered. "Please give me some time to think about it."

"All right," he smiled, "but please accept this token of our friendship." And from his pocket he brought forth a sterling silver chain to which a silver heart was attached. As he held out the gift before her, it glistened in the light of the now-descending moon. It seemed to compel her to reach out and take it. With a nervous hand, she touched it lightly. The words, "Love, Ken," were inscribed on its face. It was so beautiful in its simplicity, so significant of love, "...of our friendship," Ken had said.

She smiled tenderly and nodded slightly.

That was what Ken had been waiting for. He fastened the chain around her neck, and they started strolling away. This time, her arm also was around him. They stopped in front of the door of her cabin and reluctantly said goodnight.

Chapter 5. Dawn of a New Day

THE NEXT MORNING DAWNED bright and cheerful. Sandra, Julie, and Carolyn were staying together in the same cabin; but Julie awoke to find herself alone. Glancing at her watch, she knew the reason. Hurriedly she washed and dressed and was combing her hair when Sandra came in.

"So you finally decided to get up, huh?" teased Sandra.

Ignoring the remark, Julie just said, "And where have you been so early?"

"Oh, just out messing around mostly, I guess," Sandra answered. "Ken and I took a walk up Strawberry Creek as far as—"

"Hey, wait a minute," interrupted Julie, just noticing the chain around Sandra's neck. "Where and when and who and how?" she asked, pointing to the heart.

Sandra laughed. "It's Ken's," she replied. "We're not going steady, though"—then she added—"yet. It just means we're good friends," she explained, "really good friends. He asked me to go steady last night, but I told him I'd have to think about it. Anyway, what I came in here to tell you is—"

"Oh, sorry to interrupt you, but have you seen Carolyn?"

"Oh, yes, she's out there working on Steve."

"And how is Steve reacting?"

"Well, the normal way boys react to Carolyn Bullenhacker. But I don't think she'll go too far with Steve because he's just not that kind."

"Well, what's the news that was so important when you came in here?"

"Oh," said Sandra, "Eddy wanted me to tell you he's sorry for everything that happened last night, and he doesn't want you to be mad at him."

"Oh, really?" said Julie. "What else is new?"

"Oh, Julie, he didn't know that you didn't want graduation night brought up. He asked me why you acted so funny about it."

"And just what did you tell him?"

"I told him it wasn't fair to bring up mistakes of the past."

"What did he say?"

"He said that he really didn't expect you to kiss him last night, although he really wanted you to. He was testing you, he said. He wanted to see if you would finally give in under great pressure."

"Well, he pushed it just a little too far."

"He said he realizes that now, but he just got carried away last night."

"When did he tell you all this?"

"This morning. He tagged along after Ken and me until he made me promise I'd tell you he was sorry."

"Well, if you see him again, tell him it takes a man to apologize face to face, will you?"

Sandra smiled. "Okay. Are you coming out now?"

"In a few minutes," she said.

Five minutes later, Julie arrived at the mess hall in the lodge where the kids had gathered waiting to hear "Come and get it!" from the camp cook. She wandered over to the fireplace and was gazing at the burning logs when a gentle hand touched her shoulder. She turned to see Eddy. But before he could say anything—

"Okay, kids, breakfast's ready!" Mr. Marcos called. In the same instant, all the kids scurried to find a place in line where they each got a plate, cup, and silverware and helped themselves to the steaming hot pancakes with maple syrup and butter. From there, they found places to eat along the rows of tables and benches.

Somehow, in the crowd, Julie and Eddy got lost from each other. By the time Julie had gone through line, there wasn't room for her at the table where the rest of the gang was sitting. So she sat at the next table. All the time while she was eating, she could feel Eddy's eyes penetrating through her. He said nothing and she didn't say anything. Eddy just sat and stared.

By the time breakfast was over, Julie was a nervous wreck. When she had taken her dishes into the kitchen, she looked around for Sandra. Most of the kids were migrating outside to join the snowball fight, so she figured Sandra possibly had gone outside. She was getting ready to go outside when she heard someone call her name. She turned, and there stood Eddy. She turned back toward the door.

"Julie," he called softly. "Please don't be mad at me. About last night—I'm sorry, Julie." He paused. "I don't know what else to say, but I don't want you to go and...and..." His voice trailed off. Then, seeing the piano at hand, he sat down and played. Looking at Julie, he sang, "I'm Sorry I Made You Cry," his voice echoing in the empty hall. When he finished singing, Julie smiled warmly at him.

"Okay, Romeo," she said, "I get the point."

When they walked outside together, Ken, who stood with Sandra on the porch, remarked, "Oh, did you two kids finally make out, I mean make up?"

Julie glared at him in mock disgust. Ken laughed. "Oh," Sandra said to Julie, "are you guys going with the group at ten to Pine Cove to go sledding or are you staying here and going ice skating?"

"We're going to Pine Cove, aren't we, Eddy?" she said, looking at him.

"I guess so," he said, "but we, I mean all four of us, if we're going, had better get into the kitchen and get busy. We've got KP duty this morning, you know."

"Oh, Eddy," said Julie, "don't be so dramatic. What's a few dishes to wash?"

"A few!" exclaimed Eddy. "A hundred and twenty-seven people ate breakfast in there this morning, and you say we've got 'just a few.'"

"Well," said Julie, "what are we standing here for? Let's go get busy." She started inside and Eddy followed her.

"We'll be there in a minute," Ken called after them. When the door shut, Ken chuckled softly. "Those kids," he said, shaking his head.

"They aren't so much younger than we are, remember," Sandra said. "Julie's a freshman, and we're just sophomores."

"I know," said Ken, but they just seem so juvenile, 'cause Eddy's just an eighth grader, I guess. I don't see why Julie doesn't pick on somebody her own age."

"Well, confidentially," Sandra said, "she has an inferiority complex."

"But why should she?" asked Ken in surprise. "She's just as good as anybody in the school. And when she isn't around some squirt like Eddy, you could never tell by her actions she's not 15—or older."

"It's a long story," sighed Sandra. "Remember when Miss Delavin taught seventh grade?"

"How could I ever forget?" said Ken, throwing his hand to his head.

"Well, you came here in the last semester of that year, didn't you? At the first of the year, someone spread some nasty little rumors about Julie. I'll give you the details some other time, maybe. Anyway, Miss Delavin was Ella's second cousin, and she believed practically anything Ella and Cynthia said. You can imagine Julie had a pretty hard time. And to make things worse, Dick Clarke's dad was transferred to New York that summer. Dick had been the one who always stuck up for Julie, you know. And then, to top it all off, Miss Delavin became the eighth-grade teacher for the next year. So no wonder Julie broke down and did what she did graduation night. And ever since then, Julie's not been the same vivacious, gay girl she used to be."

Ken was silent for a moment as he stared blankly at the white ground. He nodded slightly to himself, then turned to Sandra. As though awakened out of a dream, he said, "I guess we'd better get in there and help those kids, huh?"

Chapter 6. On the Slope

HOURS LATER, DOZENS of carefree kids were at Pine Cove. Some had sleds, others pulled toboggans, and a few brave souls were trying their luck on skis. At the moment, Ken and Eddy were trying to persuade Sandra and Julie to muster up enough courage to take the half-mile toboggan ride down the hillside. Steve and Carolyn piled onto a little sled which made its way down the hillside, she displaying all the charms she could, and he trying his best to resist her and failing every minute. Jim Donaldson and JoAnn were on skis, racing down a clear mountain slope, the chilly wind blowing through long blonde wisps of hair that had escaped from under her wool cap. Ella and Cynthia were just taking a walk by themselves. Sledding, they thought, was too juvenile. And as for skiing, well, uh, they'd just rather take a walk.

Whoops! There goes Ken and Sandra and Julie and Eddy down the hill on a toboggan. Finally got up enough courage, eh, girls? Minutes later, at the bottom of the slope where the toboggan had overturned before coming to a complete halt, Sandra and Julie, red-faced and breathless, brushed the snow off themselves.

After regaining his composure, Eddy announced, "Wow, that was fun! Let's try it again."

"No, thank you," spoke Ken from where he still sat in the snow. "You kids can, but I think I've had enough for one day."

"What did you have in mind?" asked Sandra. "Going back to the camp so we can go ice skating on Strawberry Creek?"

"Yeah!" put in Julie. "That's a swell idea!"

"Well," said Ken, "not exactly. I was thinking maybe the four of us could take a little drive. We could walk back to camp first—it's not too far—and maybe you girls could fix us a lunch. And, if Mr. Marcos would let us, we could go up to Crystal Falls for a couple hours. Maybe Steve and Carolyn would like to go along, too."

"Man, where does he get all the bright ideas?" Eddy said.

"Well," continued Ken, "if it's okay with you girls, then let's take the toboggan back and go find Mr. Marcos."

"Fine with me," said Sandra.

"Sure," agreed Julie.

When they reached the top of the hill, Mr. Marcos informed them he had made no other plans for the afternoon. They could go to Crystal Falls on the condition that a responsible adult went along. At that, Ken and Sandra looked at each other. Then Julie had a thought.

"Mr. Marcos," she said, "didn't I see Paul and Donna Mott's car in the camp this morning?"

"Why, yes," said Mr. Marcos. "They drove up after breakfast this morning. Why?"

Julie looked at Ken, and Ken looked at Sandra; and they both looked back at Julie. They knew what she had in mind. Paul and Donna were a young married couple who also belonged to the RYC, as the Senior Youth Division ranged from ages 18 to 25. They were a lot of fun to be with, and they were adults, weren't they?

At that moment, who should happen by but Paul and Donna! Before Julie could answer Mr. Marcos, Ken turned to Paul and Donna with, "Say, how would you two like to go with us for a picnic this afternoon up to Crystal Falls?"

Paul and Donna looked at each other for a moment. Then Paul said, "About what time, do you know?"

"Just as soon as the girls can fix a lunch. We should be back before dark." He looked at Mr. Marcos, who looked at Paul and Donna as if to say, "Okay, Ken, it's up to them."

"Well," said Paul, looking at Donna, "how about it, honey?"

"Fine with me if you want to," she replied.

"Okay," Paul said to Ken and the others, "it's a deal!"

With Donna, Sandra, Julie, and Carolyn all helping, it did not take long to fix a little lunch. They rode up to Crystal Falls in the Motts' station wagon. Paul, Sandra, and Ken, who drove, sat in the front seat. Eddy, Julie, and Donna rode in the middle seat; Steve and Carolyn rode in the back.

The group spent a very pleasant afternoon together. They found a delightful spot in the Crystal Falls Park with a magnificent view of the falls. Beside the table where they sat, a babbling brook made its way downstream. Although the altitude here was higher than Pine Cove, because of some climatic difference, the water here was flowing freely.

Once in a while, a squirrel would timidly venture quite close to the table to see if anyone had dropped any crumbs. But soon the lunch, which the girls had thrown together in such a hurry, disappeared. It had been delicious, and the scenery here was absolutely beautiful. What more could a fellow ask for than this?

For a long while, all was pleasantly silent, the only sound being that of the icy water plunging over the cliff. Paul and Donna were reliving the first precious moments of their honeymoon as they had stood side by side at Niagara. To Ken and Sandra, it seemed like one of those storybook lands where their story would end, "...and they lived happily ever after." They possessed a mutual feeling of togetherness that only two can share. To Steve and Carolyn, it was just a background for making out. To Eddy and Julie, who were both art-minded, it was an inspiration for them to want to portray their innermost thoughts on canvas or a sheet of music paper. But all good things must end, and the afternoon passed quickly. Paul was the one to break the silence.

"It's almost five o'clock," he announced grimly. So, reluctantly, the kids stirred from their places and piled into the car.

Chapter 7. Campfire

AFTER SUPPER, MR. MARCOS built a bonfire on the bank of Strawberry Creek. In the twilight, skating forms glided across the cool, smooth ice. When the skaters grew tired, they came to rest in the glow of the flickering fire where they could roast marshmallows or join in the singing of the campfire songs accompanied by Ken on his guitar. For a long while, the silhouetted figures skating back and forth crowded the hard ice. Then, one by one, as the shadows deepened, the skaters dropped out and came to join the ever-increasing number around the bonfire.

"Why don't you and Ken come on and skate?" Julie called to Sandra once or twice as she and Eddy whizzed by the group. "It's lots of fun!"

Sandra made no reply. She didn't want to embarrass Ken in front of everyone. But when Julie stopped to rest, Sandra told her the plain truth. "Ken can't skate. He doesn't know how."

Later, when Sandra and Julie were sitting side by side, Julie looked around the group. Then she nudged Sandra.

"Are Ella and Cynthia still skating?" whispered Julie.

"No, I don't think so," answered Sandra.

"I don't see them any place, do you?"

Sandra looked around. She, too, could not see them anywhere. She looked back at Julie, who was staring blankly into the blazing fire.

Just then Julie saw a lone figure dart from behind a tree. But she said nothing because it could have been a shadow. Later, however, when Julie looked up, she saw two familiar faces in the glow of the dying coals. She nudged Sandra and nodded lightly in that direction. Sandra saw Ella and Cynthia, who had not been there before. She looked back at Julie, a suspicious look on her face. Julie returned the glance. But Ken had strummed the last chord on the lone guitar, Mr. Marcos smothered the dying coals, and Sandra and Julie made their way to their cabin.

The morning dawned all too quickly. This was the day of departure back to Riverdale. While everyone was busy packing, an atmosphere of gaiety seemed to prevail. Then, suddenly, a cry of dismay came from the little cabin.

"It's gone! It's gone!" gasped Julie.

"What's gone?" asked Sandra.

"M-my story," said Julie. "Our door was unlocked last night when we were skating, wasn't it?"

"Why, I guess so, but—"

"And remember last night when Ella and Cynthia were missing?"

"Well," said Carolyn, "what are your conclusions?"

"I'm not accusing them," said Julie, "at least not yet."

"What was the story about, anyway?" asked Sandra. She knew how Julie loved to write.

"It was really very harmless, but in the hands of Ella and Cynthia, it could be a very dangerous weapon." Julie explained, "the title of it was *One More Night*. It was about two extremely jealous rivals. The story begins in their childhood and finishes when the girls are old ladies. Anyway, some incidents were like things that have happened between Cynthia and me. One girl is a beautiful strawberry blonde and very rich. The other is a little girl from the other side of the tracks. Of course, the rich one has an advantage over the other one. In later life, the fellow whom they fight over is a rich society man. But he chooses the poor girl, and the other has a very horrible defeat."

"Oh, I see," drawled Sandra, with a very understanding look. "Are you sure you've looked every place?"

"I'm positive," Julie assured her. "The only reason I brought it with me is that I planned to stop at the house of the magazine editor who lives halfway down the hill and give it to him. They were going to publish it in the February edition of 'The World and Its People.'"

"I bet you they took it," said Carolyn.

Julie shook her head sadly. "Well, hope for the best and expect the worst."

"What are you going to do?" asked Sandra.

"I don't know," said Julie. "But just pretend you don't know anything has happened. And if you two, either of you, see anything of it, well, let me know."

Both girls nodded.

Hours later, Ken and Sandra and Eddy and Julie were in the car waiting for Steve and Carolyn. Soon Carolyn appeared, but without Steve.

"Where's Steve?" asked Ken.

"He'll be here in a minute," answered Carolyn coolly. "He's talking to Ella and Cynthia." At that statement, Ken and Eddy looked at Carolyn in surprise for taking it so lightly. But Julie and Sandra only gave her a look as if to say, "Smart thinking!"

When Steve finally came, he had a large envelope in his hand. When Eddy questioned him about it, he replied it was some kind of business letter from Dr. Donaldson for his dad. Carolyn only looked at him in her own sweet way, then settled back on the seat beside him.

Halfway down the hill, Steve spoke to Ken, who was driving. "We need to stop here," he said, pointing to Ken's left. "Turn right there on Anchor Court."

There was a small metal sign on an old building. It read "The World and Its People—Editorial Office." Julie secretly breathed a sigh of relief.

"I'll be right back," Carolyn announced, getting out of the car, envelope in hand.

"Hey, where is she going with Dr. Donaldson's letter to Steve's dad?" Eddy asked. But no one answered, so Eddy just scratched his head and shrugged.

Carolyn gave Julie a quick wink as she was coming back to the car. "Thank you," she whispered to Steve, snuggling up beside him again. But only Julie found out what Carolyn had promised Steve if he would get Julie's story from Ella and Cynthia's cabin when they were out. It would be Julie's very first published story, and she knew she would be forever grateful to Carolyn Bullenhacker.

Chapter 8. Christmas Eve in Riverdale

DAYS PASSED, AND BEFORE anyone knew it, it was almost Christmas Eve. As was the tradition, the kids met on Christmas Eve to go Christmas caroling. This year they met at the Emorys' large estate, which they called The Rolling Hills Ranch. Dr. Emory was a Professor of Dentistry at the University of Riverdale, and Mrs. Emory was a real society lady. Steve was their only son, and some even said they spoiled him. The Emorys were pretty well to do, but they were generous and pretty nice people once you got to know them.

It was a tired but happy group who arrived back at Emorys' about 11:30 for hot chocolate and gingerbread, as was the custom. Everyone gathered around the enormous fireplace in Emorys' spacious living room to sing a few of the favorite old carols before departing to their various homes.

As Julie and Sandra were going home in the latter's car through the crowded streets of Riverdale, soft white flakes fell from the sky. It was a cold, crisp night in the city. Store windows were gaily lighted and decorated, and cheery Christmas bells were jingling everywhere. Unlike in other cities, in Riverdale Christmas Eve was the only night of the year that the stores all stayed open all night long.

When the girls finally made their way out of the traffic jam, Sandra prepared to turn on Sunset Lane.

"Why don't you keep on Main Street until we get to Seventh?" asked Julie. "It's quicker than turning here."

"I know," said Sandra, "but we'd have to pass Marsha's house."

"What does that have to do with it?" asked Julie curiously.

"Well," answered Sandra sheepishly, "I don't want her to see us together. She's probably still up."

"But, why?" asked Julie, now more confused than ever.

"Well," explained Sandra. "Just don't say anything about it. Marsha doesn't quite understand the way we've been friends since fourth grade. She thinks because you're younger you should run around with kids your own age. Like Eddy. Marsha's a real nice person and a good friend, but...well, she's kind of sensitive about our friendship. Do you understand?"

Julie was silent for a moment. "Of course, Sandra," she replied softly while still looking straight ahead. *So that's why all the mystery*, Julie thought, *why Sandra never invites Marsha and me over at the same time.* Marsha had graduated last year and was now working in the Riverdale beauty shop. But she was so gay and seemed so young, as young as the kids in Sandra's class. She often came to many of the sophomore class parties. But lately Marsha had not been coming to so many things because of her job, Julie had supposed. "Oh, well," thought Julie, "here I am at home."

"Goodbye, Sandra," said Julie as she got out of the car. "Merry Christmas!"

"Merry Christmas!" returned Sandra.

Christmas day was a festive occasion for the people of Riverdale. Around four o'clock that day, Julie was washing the dishes from Christmas dinner when she saw a moving van pull up in the driveway of the empty house next door. As she watched, a man, a woman, and a girl whom Julie thought looked about her own age, emerged from the cab. When she looked again, she saw it was not really a moving van, only a large truck. The three people seemed to be dressed rather poorly. But, although their clothes were patched, they were neat and clean.

Julie resolved to herself to get better acquainted with the new family. However, she was very busy during the next week and did not have time to meet them. The next time she saw them was at church. They sat in the back row, looking very timid. Their best clothes, Julie saw, although clean and pressed, were faded and worn. But Julie bore no prejudice, and she greeted them with a warm smile. During the sermon, however, Julie could not keep her mind on the sermon for thinking of those people. She decided to talk to the pastor as soon as church was over.

Epilogue: The Big Day

Sandra smiled to herself as she watched the sleek Emory station wagon peel out of the driveway. Steve was the same ol' playboy, grown up physically, cute enough to make any girl swoon, but still as mischievous as ever. He was a flirt and a tease, but actually bashful with asking for dates. He was a college man now, but far from serious. Steve would make good, she knew, when he got over being torn between dentistry and politics. Or perhaps he would incorporate both into his life. Only time would tell.

Her thoughts drifted toward Cynthia. She hadn't changed much either—especially regarding Steve. Of course, Carolyn the "wolverine" had long since disappeared from the scene. There had been Phyllis and Diana and Suzi, and who knows who else? But for seven long years, Cynthia had not given up. Sweet, sophisticated Cynthia was still chasing Steve.

Then there was Ella. She now thought Riverdale was such a dead town, and she had gone out of state to college. Boyfriends? Sandra didn't know. But surely Ella was a part of Riverdale, and Riverdale was still a part of her. Ella would move back to California, to New City, to work as a dental hygienist. But there would always be those childhood memories of the swimming parties and hayrides and weekends at the RYC—and of Ken.

Ken! Sandra closed her eyes for a second. She had Ken's wedding invitation in her scrapbook. That RYC! It was in RYC that Ken had given her that silver heart, and it was in RYC that vivacious Gloria Martin had taken him from her. But through the months, Gloria—like

Carolyn—had disappeared. And Ken had met Rebecca. He had been only eighteen when they got married, and Sandra didn't envy Rebecca. But she was happy for Ken, now a father-to-be.

Sandra turned from her window to answer the telephone that was now ringing. Her startled expression turned to laughter as she recognized the voice on the other end.

"JoAnn Cunningham! What are you doing back in ol' Riverdale?"

The girl laughed. "Oh, Sandra, I just had to see you. I heard about the special occasion, so I came to stay the weekend with my aunt. If you could come back to Riverdale after having gone away to Pacific Christian College up north, I guess I could drive over from New City."

Sandra laughed. "JoAnn, it's been so long—nearly five years. Say, why don't you come over and we'll talk over old times?"

"Fine with me! But aren't you too busy today?"

"Oh, not now," Sandra said. "I've been in a mad rush for the past two weeks. But everything's all ready now, and I've got all afternoon."

"Okay!" agreed JoAnn. "Be right over!"

So in just ten minutes JoAnn was at Sandra's front door. When they saw each other, the surprise was even greater.

"Little Sandra with the pigtails!" JoAnn exclaimed. "Wow!"

Sandra laughed. "And what's happened to 'freckle face'?"

JoAnn stretched out her arm, smiling. "This happened."

"You're engaged!" Sandra cried. "How wonderful! Who is he?"

And so the afternoon passed, the two girls sharing plans and reminiscing about past years.

"And how are the Donaldsons?" JoAnn asked presently. "Cynthia and Jim and Bruce?"

Sandra's eyes twinkled. "Especially Jim?"

JoAnn blushed. "Well, we did spend a lot of time together the few months I lived in Riverdale. Working on the paper, going to banquets, spending time at Riverdale Youth Camp—"

"Oh, the RYC!" Sandra sighed. "Too bad Mr. Marcos got transferred. We had such good socials. But then the kids started moving away and going away to school. How are Paul and Donna Mott? Didn't they move to New City?"

"Yes, but we don't see them too often. New City's a big place. All I know is that their little girl will start Kindergarten this fall."

"Their little girl! Why, JoAnn, they were only newlyweds when they came to Riverdale. Time really flies, I guess."

"Speaking of time," JoAnn said, "look at the clock. I'd better be going. Just two hours, Sandra!"

The girls rose to their feet. "It's been a lovely afternoon, JoAnn. Thanks for stopping by."

"Thank *you*," JoAnn said. "You can meet my husband-to-be tonight when I meet yours. See you there. And, Sandra, calm down!"

Sandra giggled. "'Bye, hon."

Too excited to eat, Sandra showered and dressed and waited. Then an old scrapbook in the corner of her closet caught her eye. She sat down and thumbed through it. There were pictures of a high school banquet and very familiar faces. The snapshots were candid shots Jim had taken, and now Sandra laughed out loud at some scenes.

There was best friend Julie, perplexed and surrounded by three boys–Dennis, Billy, and Eddy. Sandra remembered that banquet well—and afterward. Julie had probably long since forgotten the dilemma of choosing between Dennis and Billy, since both fellows had disappeared from the Riverdale group. Not long after Dennis moved away, Eddy and Billy Kingston's family had moved away, too. Now they lived in Riverdale only in memory.

Julie had grown up very much since that banquet. She had known the childhood agony of young and foolish first love, the excitement of dating an "older man" when she was a high school junior, the heartbreak and insight into the problems of going steady, and the phases of retreating then "playing the field" and then beginning to settle down and grow up.

"Sandra, honey, are you ready yet?" The voice broke through her thoughts.

"Yes, Daddy," she called. "I'll be right there."

Sandra smiled inside as she walked out to the car with her new family. It had been so hard for so long after Mother died, but Sandra and her father shared a strong faith in God. Now he was happy with the new Mrs. Lee and the son he had always wanted. And, of course, he had his only daughter Sandra.

The 17-year-old boy climbed into the back seat beside his stepsister. "Hey, Sandra, why does an elephant have flat feet?"

Sandra looked at her little stepbrother Joe. "From jumping out of trees," she answered in mock nonchalance. "Why does an elephant wear tennis shoes?"

"Because he has flat feet," Joe returned. "And he floats downstream on his back so he won't get his tennis shoes wet, and you can tell if an elephant's in your bathtub because you can smell peanuts on his breath."

Sandra sighed, looking at Joe from the corner of her eye, trying hard not to laugh.

Joe giggled. "Now that I've wrecked all your elephant jokes—"

"Oh, yeah?" she retorted. "How do you get down from an elephant?"

It stumped Joe. "Aw, come on, sis, tell me!" he pleaded.

"After the honeymoon," she teased.

While Sandra waited for Julie to arrive in the bridal room at the church, her mind wandered again. Riverdale, like the people who lived in it, had changed, too. The "little kids" who once had been so unimportant to Riverdale were now the center of everything. There was Cynthia's younger brother Bruce, Ella's little brother Frank and sister Judy, and many more who had moved in and grown up. Beth and Fred and Carole and—Sandra couldn't possibly name them all.

At that moment, Julie appeared, duly excited. "Well, Sandra, it's almost time for the big moment!"

Sandra could not hide the anticipation. "Oh, Julie!"

"Oh, yes, I meant to tell you—Marsha's here with Larry!"

"Oh? Did you talk to her?" Sandra remembered for an instant the trivial childhood jealousies she had forgotten long ago.

"Just for a few minutes. She was so sorry I wasn't able to go to her wedding, but I told her you said it was beautiful."

"Speaking of weddings, Julie, didn't Sarah get married recently?"

"Yes," Julie answered, "she married a very fine Christian man. I'm thrilled for her. You know, everybody worried about her for such a long time. But no one could blame her much for running away from home—if you could call it a home. She's had such a hard time in life. I'll never forget that Christmas when they moved to Riverdale, right next door to us—"

Sandra nudged her. "Excuse me, but isn't that Darlene?"

Julie looked. "Say, it is! And that's Dr. Smith's son she's with! She's doing pretty well, I guess."

Sandra smiled. Then she sighed. "Oh, Julie, just think. In just a few minutes, Bob will stand up there on the platform just waiting for his bride..."

"Oh, Sandra! How could things be any more perfect? You know, when I first met Allen at Highview, I had wanted to be a minister's wife for as long as I could remember. And we made all those plans for when Allen and Bob would finish seminary then the four of us would be an evangelistic team. But I never dreamed that I would meet my best friend and soulmate, Howard, at La Paloma College, much less be getting married to him this summer. God has been so good to us both. Sandra, we're the luckiest women in the whole wide world!

"Julie, our cue's coming pretty quick," Sandra whispered. "This is it!"

It was just a few seconds until the *Wedding March* would begin; but in that few seconds, Sandra's life seemed to pass through her mind. The summer after Ken, there had been LeRoy Chester who moved next door. They, too, had planned to marry—until he moved away. He was gone completely from Riverdale and from Sandra's heart. Then there had been George, rich and romantic. George's wedding had been two years ago.

Then there was the schoolteacher, Raymond Pierce, eleven years older but full of life and living it to the fullest. He had proposed to Sandra and promised her a nice home, prestige, and a way through college with all the trimmings. To Sandra, it was wild and exciting, but not exactly what she wanted to live with 24 hours a day.

But it was through Raymond that Sandra had met Bob Miller, the Bob she was going to marry today. She remembered the Christmas Eve they spent with Allen and Julie and the plans they had made for their years at college and seminary and the evangelistic team, but especially for Sandra and Bob's life together for God. Of course, their courtship and engagement had been long. She had even had a brief fling with Kurt Gaston and Bill Johnson, who had been so much a part of Riverdale. And, of course, things had changed a lot for Julie, too. She had finally gotten over Allen Macintosh and had found the love of her life in Howard Davidson.

Now Sandra and Julie were grown-up women, not little girls of Riverdale. The *Wedding March* had begun, and Julie as maid of honor had started down the aisle. A little nervously, Sandra smiled at her father and took his arm. Then they started down the aisle toward the minister on the platform where Bob stood, waiting for his bride....

NOVEMBER RAIN

A mini-novella describes the first relationship of main character Julie Scott with boyfriend Allen Macintosh, a character who will appear again and again throughout the series. Both are attending a private Christian day school, Highview Academy, in a town 35 miles away from Riverdale. Allen and Julie's first date is to a concert at nearby La Paloma College in November 1960.

The Acquaintance

"I SURE WISH WE DIDN'T have to move." Eloise stared down at the dusty road, partly to shade her eyes from the August sun which beat down upon the girls, and partly because of the fact of her statement.

"Yes, it's too bad. Just when you get to know someone, it seems, they have to move," said the older dark-haired girl. "It's a shame they have to transfer our ministers so often. Who *is* the new pastor, anyway?"

"Macintosh, I think Daddy said."

"Do they have any kids, these Mac— Mac —What was the name?"

"Macintosh," repeated Eloise. "I think they have some boys about your age." Her eyes were teasing.

"Really?" Julie's eyes twinkled. Ever since June when Eddy had moved away, she had been lonely. She still remembered that last hayride.

"I don't know," shrugged Eloise. "I was just kidding you."

Julie smiled even now as she recalled that scene, one of the last times she had spent with Eloise before the Tibbses had moved to Ocean City. Now Julie checked her errand list and entered the door of the five-and-ten, Sprouse-Reitz.

"Hi, Julia!" greeted a pleasant redhead.

"Oh, hi, Ella," Julie returned. "What are you doing here?"

"Just getting some things for Mom," Ella answered. "Say, have you met the Macintoshes?"

"Oh, are they in Riverdale now?"

"Yes, they were at prayer meeting last night. Pastor Macintosh is pretty nice, and Mrs. Macintosh is the sweetest person you could ever want to know. They've got three boys, but they weren't there last night."

"*Three* boys!" Julie was afraid to ask their ages.

"Yes. I hear the oldest boy—Allen, I think is his name—is going to Highview Academy." Ella turned quickly. "Oh, there's Mom! See you tomorrow night."

Allen Macintosh—that was an unfamiliar name, at least in the Riverdale gang. *Highview Academy, huh? I wonder what he's like.* But tomorrow night soon came.

He stood there all alone in the church's hallway, looking through the window into the sanctuary. His blond hair, not cut short like most of the fellows', was the first thing Julie noticed besides the neat blue suit he wore. And he wore glasses. "Probably the intellectual-type snob," she thought. Then she hurried on inside to play the organ.

Allen could see her at the organ and soon heard her play. "She isn't too pretty," he thought, "but she plays well."

The following day at church was the beginning of Julie's acquaintance with the Macintoshes. Mrs. Macintosh *was* a sweet person. The two younger ones, Peter and Kenny, were typical boys. The pastor was a very congenial and handsome man. He and his family were recent converts from another popular Protestant denomination. His sermon that day was a "let's-get-acquainted" as he told his story from the time of his teenage conversion and his restless longing, searching for truth until the present time. It was a wonderfully touching story to hear, and Julie's eyes were not dry as the congregation sang the closing hymn. And thus was her first great impression of the Macintosh family.

"Julie, isn't the new minister's son—what's his name?—Allen? Isn't he supposed to be here tonight?" Sandra nudged her friend.

"I think so," the other girl shrugged. Just then a station wagon pulled into the driveway and Julie heard familiar voices.

The teenagers, gathered at Ken Nelson's folks' farm, were eager to get started on the hayride. All the kids were there except Cynthia and her two brothers—and Allen Macintosh.

Now Cynthia appeared in the doorway with a cheery greeting and an apology for being late. Then, turning toward the boy who followed her, she announced, "Hey, kids, you know Allen, don't you? Allen, you know Ella and my brothers, there's Butch and Carlos, here's Sandra and Julie and Ken..." She pointed to each one as she continued on around the room calling out each name.

"And here's Steve!" bellowed a voice from the kitchen. The kids laughed to see the handsome, popular "life of the party" gulping down a cookie that just couldn't wait for later.

Allen smiled, too. "Hello, Steve," he said.

The Riverdale Youth Club social was a success. After the hayride, there were refreshments then a volleyball game in Nelsons' driveway until, one by one, the teenagers went home.

Julie, timid and insecure, couldn't help feeling just a little lonely since best friend Sandra was with LeRoy. With the full August moon above her, Julie half-wished Eddy hadn't moved away. Then, from a distance, she got a good look at the new minister's oldest son. He sure looked different in a T-shirt and jeans than he had in his suit. *He must be about 14 if he's a freshman. And why did he come tonight with Cynthia?* But soon it was over, the weekend had passed, and school was about to begin.

The first day of school dawned bright and early, but Julie was up before the sun. There was that piano to practice. Then came the thrill of first climbing into the Emorys' station wagon on a crisp autumn morning with all five or six books in one's arms. This was Mrs. Emory's last year at the dental hygiene school in Highview. Perhaps Steve, being sixteen next year, would drive to La Paloma Prep School for his junior year. Perhaps...but Julie determined to enjoy the present and not worry about the future.

If Julie were timid and insecure, Allen could not detect it. *After all, wasn't she going with the playboy, Steve?* This thought ran through Allen's mind along with other confused things as he dressed for school. He shivered a bit—half from the chill of the early morning and half from the excitement of something new and unknown—as he waited on the corner. Then he saw the gray station wagon that pulled over to the curb.

But as he got into the car, it surprised Allen to see only Steve, his mom, and little sister Sharon in the front. So Carlos, Julie, and Allen sat in the back. *Is Julie going with Steve?*

"Good morning, Mrs. Emory," he greeted cheerily as he got in and closed the door. "And Steve, Carlos, Sharon, and Julie." She smiled in recognition when he spoke her name. And she mentally noted his mannerly courtesy.

After the first few miles of normal chatter, silence grew. Allen settled back to relax and thought about the day ahead of him and this new way of life. It was his first day in high school, his first year in a Christian academy. He no longer missed the movies and school dances and pork chops on Sunday, at least not as much. He was a young Christian struggling to grow toward perfection, and he had a new vision of what God expected of him—his very best.

He would be a minister or a teacher, perhaps a teacher like Mr. Van Dyunen of his eighth-grade year. That was a good year. The scenes of his lovely eighth-grade graduation barely three months ago were still fresh in his memory. He remembered pretty dark-haired Nancy, the girl who lived up to the high standards he now believed in and made his own. And before that, in Arizona, was Jonelle he had met at the camp meeting where he first found his Lord. *I wonder if all Christian girls are the same.* He glanced at Julie. *Well, there was always Cynthia. But if only she wasn't going away to boarding school at San Margo Academy. Well, that's life. That's a common saying, but what is life, really?* Life right now meant school as the faded yellow building loomed up in the distance.

So this is Highview! It was an adventurous day. For Steve, little Sharon, and Julie, it would be a renewal of old friendships with other Riverdale High students who had transferred to Highview Academy. For Carlos and Allen, both freshmen, it would be an introduction to new young people and teachers and a new classroom routine. With the passing days, the familiarity grew until school was well under way for another year.

A Friendship Begins

THE WEEKS PASSED, AND soon the schedule of getting up early and getting home late was a routine. The Macintoshes moved into a new house on the corner of Gilbert Street where Julie lived nine blocks away. Now Allen waited for Mrs. Emory on the corner of Devonshire and Gilbert Street, where Julie also waited.

Soon Allen concluded that Julie and Steve *weren't* going together, although she surely must still like such a handsome fellow as he. And Allen wasn't sure he could really blame Steve for liking Julie—if he ever had.

There was one unique feature of the program of the six who attended school in Highview—the town was located 35 miles from Riverdale, the longest distance any of the students had to travel. This meant leaving home at 7:15 a.m. and returning home after five every night except Friday. And because of Mrs. Emory's class schedule, this also meant breakfast in the Highview College Cafeteria on Monday mornings. But the kids did their homework after school in the College library. It was normal for the five to study at the same table: brilliant, unoccupied, mischief-loving Carlos; handsome, quick-tempered, good-natured Steve; studious, timid, and self-conscious Julie; this new personality, Allen; and Sharon, who after a short time, because of her restless lively energies, went to a babysitter's after school.

One particular afternoon, Allen and Julie just sat across from each other at the study table for the first time, but not the last. Engaged in a low-toned informal conversation, the two grew better acquainted, as is the natural course. Allen discovered that beneath her quiet reserve, Julie could be quite a friendly girl. And she discovered that although this pastor's son was different, he was a real wit and a ball to be with.

Then Julie left for home right after school on Mondays because of a music lesson. But Allen, who had made friends with Steve and Carlos, scarcely missed her until one day she spoke to him.

"Would you like a ride home early? My folks are here," she said.

Allen thought a minute. "What about the other boys?"

"Steve would rather wait for his mom," Julie continued, "and Carlos wants to stay with him."

It really didn't matter to Allen how he got home, but the sooner the better. "Okay. Thanks," he said hastily and followed her to the car.

But Monday after Monday, Allen continued to accept Julie's invitation. Then came that weekend, that Riverdale Youth Club campout at Pine Cove.

Dr. and Mrs. Emory were excellent as the RYC sponsors. The food was terrific, and the well-planned activities were spectacular. Perhaps Allen's younger brother Peter noticed more than Allen did that quite a few couples existed among the group. But Allen, too, silently watched.

Riding up to the mountain campsite late in the afternoon in the back of Emorys' truck, couples snuggled together because it was chilly. Peter had teased Allen, who became provoked, and Julie, who had turned red; but now Allen secretly observed her. There would be time, he figured, in the weeks to come to get to know Julie.

Mornings passed and mornings grew colder. And morning after morning Julie and Allen came from opposite directions and met at the gas station on the corner of Gilbert Street and Florida Avenue to wait for Mrs. Emory. This crisp cool October morning Julie's books lay on the cash box and Allen's books balanced on the hood of his father's Simca parked approximately 15 feet from where they stood.

The two stood watching the western horizon when suddenly Allen started. "Hey, here they come!"

Julie looked up. Sure enough, the gray station wagon was rolling through the mist. By this time, Allen had turned and headed for the cash box.

"Your books are on the car," Julie said, thinking he had forgotten.

He stopped and flushed slightly. "Oh, I was just going to get yours for you," he blurted.

"Oh." Now it was Julie's turn to blush. But Emorys had arrived, so there was no time for debate. And each grabbed their own books and scrambled to the car.

If Julie had suspected what was going on in Allen's mind, she might have acted differently. But she soon forgot this simple incident.

"So," said Sandra over the phone the next night, "you're almost 14, huh?"

"Just two more days!" affirmed her friend.

"Well, Julie—'sweet fourteen and never been kissed," she teased. "Allen will have to do something about that!"

Julie laughed, then said, "Oh, no. Allen isn't that kind of guy. Anyway, we'll probably be nothing more than just casual friends. After all, he *is* the pastor's son!"

"Well, I don't know," drawled Sandra. "After what happened yesterday with your books—"

"Oh," Julie interrupted, "that was nothing but an act of courtesy. Nothing in the way of romance will ever happen between *us*."

Sandra said no more.

Then Julie turned 14 on a Monday afternoon. By now, Allen and Julie felt quite at ease in talking to each other.

Prior to this, Allen had noticed that Julie wrote a lot in the car instead of taking part in the boys' conversation or listening to the radio or just plain enjoying the scenery (which, after several weeks, had grown quite familiar). After some time, he found out that what she wrote was stories, fiction or nonfiction, it made no difference as long as there was a girl, a boy, and a good plot. Allen had read some of her stories and became intrigued. This curiosity led to the general drift of the conversation that Monday afternoon. But somehow Julie got off on a tangent.

"You mean you write stories just for fun?" Allen asked.

She nodded.

"Well," he said, "where do you get all the ideas?"

She shrugged. "Oh, I get inspirations from my own experiences and from my friends' experiences." She laughed. "I remember the first story I ever wrote—'The Luckiest Girl in Town.'"

"Oh?" he said, laughing with her.

But the smile disappeared from her face. And somehow it slipped out, the story of her jealousy of Cynthia and Steve and their grade-school romance.

Now Allen understood. And somehow the fact that Julie had involuntarily taken Allen into her confidence made Allen want to understand her better.

Now Julie noticed little things more and more—the way he would always tell her how good her organ music was, the time he sat beside her in church, and the times he phoned for unimportant reasons. Then came the Week of Prayer at Highview Academy that directed the course of things for Allen and Julie.

"Looking at Life"—that was the theme of the thought-provoking informal talks presented in a teenager's language by Dean Alexander from nearby La Paloma College. This week was a turning point in many lives, including Julie's. She had been a Christian most of her life, but lately it seemed she had been almost asleep spiritually. But something happened in Julie's life as she made one of the most important decisions of her entire life—her decision for God. And in the days that followed, even Allen noticed the change. Julie was a dedicated Christian, the kind of Christian he wanted for a close friend.

It was November, and the weather was quite chilly. But to Julie everything seemed like spring—wonderful, exuberant, and unexplainable. Maybe it was her vows to God. Maybe it was a secret looking-forward-to of Monday afternoons. Maybe it was a subconscious intuition that something big might happen....

"Say, wasn't that an excellent program today?" Julie asked casually that November Monday.

"Yes, it was," agreed Allen. "La Paloma College orchestra, huh? They're pretty good. Are you going to their concert Saturday night?"

"Oh, I'd love to!" she said, thinking only of the music. "But," her countenance fell, "La Paloma's so far away from Riverdale, and I know my folks won't take me that late at night."

"I'd like to go, too," Allen said. "Maybe I can get my folks to go. Would you like to go?" The question was casual, but for a moment their eyes met, and the magic sparkle seemed to spell one word—date.

"I'd be delighted!" she almost breathed. Looking out the window behind Allen, she said, "I-I'll let you know."

November Rain

IT WAS WEDNESDAY MORNING when Allen told Julie that his folks were going to La Paloma Saturday night. "Could you go?" he asked.

Julie wanted very much to say "yes," but she quietly replied, "I don't know for sure now. I'll let you know Friday night, okay?"

Friday night came. As usual, Allen was the first to tell Julie he liked her organ playing. Then, "Tomorrow night?" he asked.

"We may go to visit my cousins," she answered gingerly. "I'll call you."

So Allen waited. And waited until the next afternoon when he could wait no longer. He picked up the phone and dialed a number.

"Yes, Allen, I'll go with you tonight," was music to his ears.

"Fine, Julie!" Allen sighed inside. "I'll see you about six, okay?"

But six o'clock came. And Allen, Peter, and Mrs. Macintosh were at Emorys' house visiting. Allen looked at his watch nervously, although his mother knew what was going on in his mind. But Emorys weren't people one could just leave.

"How would you like to go over to La Paloma with us to a concert tonight, Steve?" Mrs. Macintosh asked.

So when Allen finally knocked on the door of Julie's house, where she had been ready for a half hour, they were on their way. *Some "date,"* Allen thought—*escorted by Mother, with best friend and little brother along!* But once Allen and Julie were together, it didn't really seem to matter.

This was so new and exciting for Julie. And everything was happening so fast. Ever since grade school days and Riverdale and Eddy and graduation night, life had been uneventful. Now she wondered if she could be good enough company for Allen to want to go with again. And again.

But Allen never knew what Julie was thinking. The night was pleasant, the melodious strains of wonderful music floated lightly through the silent hall, and an attentive, prettily shy girl sat by his side. And he was enjoying it all.

Soon, too soon, the program was over. And Allen, Julie, Steve, Peter, and Mrs. Macintosh started toward the car. But the clear November skies had clouded over, a chilly breeze rustled, and they felt a light drizzle. November rain! The first rain of the season!

"Oh, my hair!" Julie exclaimed almost delightedly.

Spotting a newspaper under a tree, Mrs. Macintosh picked it up and divided it with Julie to hold over their heads. "Here, let me do that," Allen offered, taking the paper. And together they walked out to the car.

A tired but happy couple was glad to see the lights of Riverdale. Mrs. Macintosh left Steve off at his ranch. Then there were three more miles to Julie's house. Silently and quickly Julie felt a soft warm hand over hers. Her eyes met Allen's, capturing the magic sparkle as if to echo the words of the popular song, "'Somethin' good'll come from this.'"

It was still raining when the Simca stopped at Julie's house. Allen was *so* sleepy—and quite embarrassed when his mom had to say, "Why, Allen, walk Julie to the door." And it was all Julie could do to conceal a little giggle.

But once out of the reach of the car's parking lights, Allen slipped his arm lightly around Julie's waist.

"Thank you," she said at the door. "Good night."

But "good night" did not mean "goodbye."

Early Sunday afternoon Julie's phone was ringing, and Allen was on the line.

"I just wondered if you have any poems I might use in my scrapbook for my English project," he said.

"Oh, yes. You asked me about that last Friday, didn't you?" Julie recalled. "I think I said I'd try to bring some to you tomorrow, didn't I?"

Perhaps Allen thought Julie had a poor memory. But he said, "Well, I had to have an excuse to phone you!"

To Julie, this was the first sign she might mean something special to Allen.

Monday came and was soon over. Nowhere but in Riverdale Valley were November evenings so beautiful. The long ride each day and the waiting after school grew monotonous. But to Allen and Julie, to travel those last few miles over the rolling hills planted in wheat and melons and watch the road like a long black ribbon stretching around the purple hills and past picturesque farms and cottages, then to glimpse the tall slender palm trees on the outskirts of Riverdale silhouetted against the inspiring November sunset—all this seemed to compensate for the long day. And, one by one, glittering stars appeared in the velvety sky. And a particular one in the southwestern sky seemed to glow brighter than any of the others.

"Venus!" Julie whispered delightedly.

"Starlight, star bright..." Allen replied with a tender smile. And once again, Julie felt a soft warm hand over her own.

Teenage Romance or Realism

EXCITEMENT FILLED THE crisp morning air as the students of Highview boarded the buses soon en route to Irving Park for the annual school picnic. Julie, especially, wondered about what this day might be like. Allen was sitting beside her, and she knew they had not been unnoticed. And Julie's new pride didn't cease as the day passed. They were in activities together. Even the splattered yolk on her white shoe from Allen's getting too nervous in the egg-throwing contest didn't matter. Julie loved every moment.

Later in the afternoon, Allen and Julie were just walking around when he dared to take her hand. But no sooner had he done so with an air of confidence than she slipped it out. "Mr. Wesley," she said in a low voice.

Allen looked around in embarrassment. *But teacher or no teacher,* Allen wondered. *Was that the real reason?*

But it was a proud and happy Julie who boarded the bus that afternoon with egg on her shoe, Allen's watch dangling on her arm, and many beautiful memories to treasure.

The days passed, and Allen and Julie felt they belonged together more and more. There seemed to be something new and exciting every day—a rainbow or a cloud—but Allen and Julie shared it.

Everything was so perfect. Allen and Julie could be together every day, to talk, to share their ideas and dreams. Then every weekend was special, too, just because they were special to each other. There was Young People's meeting and church when Allen and Julie could worship together, sharing a simple faith. Then the afternoon walks, hand in hand, through the country streets of Riverdale. And when Saturday night came, Allen and Julie were together again.

It was at a church social when Allen and Julie sat with Cynthia and Steve. During the moving picture, Allen quietly took Julie's hand. But she was afraid. *Not at a church social, Allen. What will they say?*

But Steve and Cynthia had already gone outside to play basketball with the younger kids. Allen and Julie went out, too. Soon, however, interest in the basketball game faded, and it left only the four of them.

"Oh, let's not quit now," Steve said. "Come on, Allen, you and Julie against Cynthia and me—'Lovers' Teams!" And so the evening passed. But Allen did not forget what Steve had said. Allen knew they accepted him and Julie as a couple.

But all too soon the honey and roses wilted. Allen's eyes filled with stars, seeing no girl but Julie. He looked forward every day to riding to school beside her in Emorys' car. But one morning when Emorys arrived at the corner, Steve and Carlos sat in the back. So Julie climbed into the front, leaving Allen to sit in the back without her. Allen said nothing then, but it deflated his ego just a little. *What could he do to prove to Julie that he really liked her?*

The day could not pass fast enough. And the minutes after school seemed to drag. Where *was* Julie? Just then her best friend at Highview passed.

"Bobbie!" Allen called. "Where's Julie?"

"Oh." Bobbie smiled warmly. "You're waiting for her?"

Allen nodded. "I suppose she's already gone?"

"No, I think she's just fooling around some place. I'll go see if I can find her and tell her you're waiting for her."

"Well, I-I—" But Bobbie disappeared.

In a few minutes, Julie appeared. Together they walked to the College library as usual. Then Allen said, "Julie?"

At first she did not sense the tenseness in his voice. "Yes, Allen?"

"Why did you ask Steve to sit in the back seat this morning?"

Julie started. "I didn't, Allen!" But why *had* Steve sat in the back seat, instead of in front with his mother and sister, as usual? It wasn't long before they found out.

Arriving at Emorys' car, a very facetious Steve, Carlos, and Sharon greeted the two. Giving a couple of young lovers a bad time might be inevitable, but Allen didn't like it. *What right do they have to intrude?* Allen should have expected more, much more. But, for the present, his security was in Julie.

Julie, too, found her security in her relationship with Allen. When the kids gave her a rough time, she always knew Allen would understand. After a Saturday night party at Macintoshes' house, Julie had sat down to play the piano when Allen snuggled up beside her.

"Play this," he said, placing sheet music in front of her. She played, and they sang it softly.

"Our song," he whispered, holding her close. "'My Happiness.'"

Every afternoon Mrs. Emory let Allen and Julie off on the corner right across the street where they met every morning, and where another gas station stood. But every afternoon the goodbyes took longer and longer to say. And soon a half hour seemed like only a few minutes.

One day Allen seemed quieter than usual. *I hope he isn't mad at me,* Julie thought.

She spoke kindly. "What is it, Allen?"

"Nothing," he replied, looking down. *I don't want to tell you, Julie.* But he looked at her questioning face, her brown eyes reflecting her wonder. "You aren't mad at me, are you, Julie?"

"No, of course not," she smiled a little. "I thought you...well, why should I be?"

He shrugged. "I don't know, Julie. I guess I've been acting dumb today." Now he would not let his eyes meet hers. "You might as well know. Mr. Conrad had a talk with me."

"Oh." Julie's smiled faded. "About—us?"

"It was nothing, really, I guess. Mostly teasing and stuff. But in front of the fellows in the shop. Especially Otto and Karl." He looked at her now. "They give us enough trouble at school."

"Oh, I know." Julie smiled in sympathy now. "But at least Mr. Conrad wasn't mad, was he?"

"No, not exactly. It's just—" Allen shook his head. "Oh, forget it, Julie! I-I'm sorry."

Julie said no more.

But Allen's turn to be sympathetic soon came. In the College library after school, Julie had gone to lie down in the ladies' lounge. Allen missed her smile from across the study table. "I'm tired," she had said, but was that all? Allen seemed to sense there was something more.

Five o'clock came, and the kids picked up their books and started toward the parking lot. But Allen refused to let Julie carry her books.

"I'll take them," she said weakly. "I-I'm all right."

"No!" Allen was firm. "Don't argue with me!"

But Allen wondered as he sat in the car waiting for Mrs. Emory. There sat his Julie, laughing and talking gaily with Steve, much more than usual. Then, at the corner gas station, it was the same quiet Julie who stood talking to baffled Allen.

"What's wrong, Julie?" he finally asked. "Aren't you feeling well?"

"I'm just a little tired," she said.

Allen took her hand. "Julie, may I ask you something?"

"Go ahead, Allen."

"But—but please don't be offended—or even feel you have to answer—"

"What is it, Allen?"

"You still like Steve, don't you?"

"Steve is a very nice person, Allen."

"Yes, I know he is. And I don't blame you—"

"But"—she paused only briefly—"not as nice as you."

Allen sighed just a little as he put his arm around Julie and squeezed her. "Oh, Julie, you don't have to say that just to make me feel good."

"I mean it, Allen."

Just then a black Simca appeared, and Allen jumped a little. "My mother!" he said.

"Hi, Mrs. Macintosh!" Julie called, feeling just a little foolish.

"Hi, Julie!" Mrs. Macintosh returned. Then, "Ready to go home, son? I called Julie's house to see if you were there."

Allen, also feeling foolish, said nothing except, "Goodbye, Julie," as he climbed into the car.

But the discussion was unfinished. "There are lots of things I'd like to know, Julie," Allen said the next day. "But I don't want to put it into words. It sounds pretty stupid."

"Don't be afraid to talk to me," Julie said. "I'll understand."

Finally, Allen wrote three questions in a note. And it was at the corner gas station when Julie tried to answer them.

"My folks didn't say too much about last night except I should have been doing my homework," she began. Then, "Allen, I think a *lot* of you. There is absolutely nothing between Steve and me. A sixth-grade romance." She laughed.

Allen smiled. "Okay, Julie," he whispered. "Okay."

The days passed. One evening Allen said, "Julie, I've lost my English book. Do you have yours from last year?"

"Yeah, I'll bring it tomorrow."

"Oh," Allen interjected, "I'll walk home with you tonight and get it if—if it's okay."

"Sure!" And so began the tradition of Allen walking Julie home every night and carrying her books every day.

But the talking and teasing of Allen and Julie had not stopped. The half hours at the gas station had become hours. The starry-eyed romanticism—plus their understanding of each other—had grown. But the antagonism from Carlos and Steve, and especially from Otto and

Karl, grew. And Allen's occasional moodiness came at the wrong times. It was late one Friday night, after an especially awful week, that Allen wrote a letter.

He had talked about this to Julie before. "That Otto and Karl really don't know when to stop teasing, do they?" Julie had observed.

Allen shook his head almost hopelessly. "It's not only them, Julie. It's all over school! Why do they talk about us like this?"

"Well," Julie tried to rationalize, "I guess most couples get talked about, eventually."

"But we have done nothing to deserve it!" Allen defended. "Why is the gossip just about one couple—you and me?"

"Is it?"

"Yes! What right do they have to do it?"

Julie, too, had shaken her head. Now Allen wrote, "Julie, even though my father has reasoned things out with me, I still have somewhat of a feeling of anxiety." And then, "You know, Julie, you're the first girl I think I ever *really* liked—with all my heart—and it's wonderful to have a girlfriend like you that really, really understands me. Yes, you're the one I'm sure I can always trust...."

To Julie, that letter was worth more than gold. Somehow she had to let Allen know how much she appreciated him, too.

Then after church Allen invited Julie home with him, the first of many, many times that Julie would eat with the Macintoshes. That day, too, was very special because Allen and Julie were together working for God. In the afternoon, they went on the usual young people's singing bands, visiting shut-ins.

Then that night they went Christmas caroling, going from door to door collecting funds for missions. And Julie did everything she could to tell Allen in a thousand little ways how much she really liked him.

"You're wonderful!" Allen kept whispering into her ear as he hugged her tightly....

But when the weekend was over, Julie sat down to answer Allen's letter. She felt guilty. They *had* gone too far Saturday night. Why did she ever let herself get out of control? Why, letting Allen put his arms around her right in front of Ella's mother and the other church people! And the way he had snuggled up in the car! She knew she must never let it happen again. She tried her best to put her feelings into words as she wrote to Allen.

Their relationship was the same; but in a day or two, Allen gave her his reply:

"There is no reason in the world for you to feel 'wicked'—I'm the one who should take all the blame. And I'm sorry...

"You said you felt that Saturday night was your fault because you were afraid to say 'no.' I disagree with you on this point (now this is what's harder to put into words!)—but don't ever be afraid to tell me 'no'!

"What is your view now (as of 6:30, December 12, 1960) about holding hands; about the times I put my arm around you Saturday night; what exactly did you think when I first put my arm around you?

"And also, you've never told me just how you feel about going steady.

"Oh, yes, one more thing. I think you're pretty, even if you don't think so."

It was in that weekend that Allen and Julie grew up. They narrowed the gap that had been between them before. They could really talk things over, to talk about their growing affection. And Allen and Julie, each in their own mind, began to ask the question that neither dared say out loud: *Could this be love?*

Could This Be Love?

THE NEXT WEEKEND FOUND the Riverdale youth on Mexico's border. It was the annual Youth Congress held at the mission school in Calexico, just on the northern side of the border. Many young people from all of southern California had come for inspiration and a little deeper insight into mission work. Among them were Allen and Julie.

Such an experience! The meetings were wonderful—God was so near—and Allen and Julie shared it all. They went with a group to a boys' home in Mexico where they sang songs and gave Christmas packages. Then Allen and Julie ate their supper together in the plaza, or park, just at sunset.

But about halfway through the meeting that evening, Allen and Julie and two others, Gloria and Ken, went on an excursion in downtown Calexico. The streets were all decorated in Christmas fashion, and bright signs of "Feliz Navidad" were everywhere. Neither Allen nor Julie felt exactly right about ditching the meeting, but for a while neither spoke.

Then Julie said, "Allen, we shouldn't have come."

Allen, who wasn't acting as gay as he had when they first started out, looked at her. "You know, Julie, that's just what I was thinking. Let's go back."

"But Gloria and Ken—"

"Hey, kids!" Allen called to the couple ahead of them. "Don't you think we should go back?"

"Oh, we just got started!" exclaimed Gloria gaily. "Not now!"

"But—" Julie spoke.

"You two go on if you want to," Ken said.

"Well—" Allen and Julie looked at each other and then back at Ken. They hesitated. But they both knew what was right.

"Okay," Allen said, "we'll see you back at the school."

And with lighter hearts, the two started back. High above the town of Calexico, the moon glowed in a sky full of stars just for Allen and Julie. On the way back, they passed a magnificent old Spanish mansion made from white stone. And from somewhere in the shadows, someone strummed a lone guitar. Neither spoke for a long while, and Allen held Julie's hand tightly in his own.

"Julie, will you go steady with me?" Allen whispered at last.

Arriving back at the meeting, they heard the strains of the closing song, sung by the mission school chorus, floating through the quiet night. "Mas alla del sol..." "Far beyond the sun..." Standing in the back door of the auditorium, Allen and Julie hummed it softly while they blinked back the tears.

Morning came and the Riverdale youth were really excited. They were going Christmas shopping across the border in Mexico!

"Gloria," Julie said to her as they were getting dressed, "I want to get Allen a real Mexican wallet for Christmas, but how can I if he's with me all day?"

"I know," said Gloria, who was just as excited, "you let me 'borrow' the money to get Ken a wallet. Of course, Allen will be with us. And when we're in a leather shop, I'll just ask him to help me pick out a wallet for Ken. And won't he be surprised on Christmas morning to find out he picked out his own present!"

"Ooh!" squealed Julie with a delighted giggle. "Okay!"

And so the "inseparable three"—Allen, Julie, and Gloria—had a wonderful time in Mexicali that Sunday. Gloria purchased the wallet with Julie's money, and Julie was happy. Allen was happy, too, because he had figured out Julie and Gloria's little scheme. *She thinks I'll be surprised,* he thought. *Just wait until Christmas Eve!* And he thought again of the present he already had for her.

Coming home in Macintoshes' car that afternoon, Allen and Julie were filled with an ecstasy that only young and first love knows. His arm was around her, and they sat in silence, basking in the warmth of their embrace. She was close enough to kiss. Should he? He touched his lips to her cheek, but then he pulled away. No. But didn't he love her? He knew he admired and respected her very much. Now he pressed his cheek lightly against her own. He was sure....

It wasn't easy to get back into the school routine for just one week before Christmas vacation. But if Allen had moods, so did Julie. It was the last day of school before vacation, and Julie snapped at her parents in front of Allen. She immediately felt bad. When she was alone with Allen, she broke down and cried on his shoulder. Allen understood.

"Oh, Allen!" she sobbed, shaking her head. "Why, why am I so awful?"

He patted her gently. "Julie," he whispered. "Nobody's perfect."

"But I'm so far from it! I—I guess I'm just too worried."

"About what?" He squeezed her hand.

But she only sobbed and shook her head.

"Look, Julie," he said. "If you're really troubled, why don't you talk to my dad?"

Julie looked blankly at him. *Your dad? A minister? Never!* "I—I couldn't," she stammered.

"Why not?" he queried. "Dad's a wonderful person to talk to—to understand you. I've done it and—"

"But you're different! You're their son."

"But he and Mom like you a lot, Julie. They would be so happy to know you trust them, too. Give it a try."

Julie started thinking. Meanwhile, she forgot her tears. Pastor Macintosh—understanding—wonderful to talk to. Well, if he was anything like his son... Why should she be afraid to talk to a minister, anyway?

"I'll go with you," Allen was saying. "That is—if you want me to."

Julie only looked as if she were going to speak, but she didn't.

"Well, think about it," Allen whispered.

Julie *would* think about it. Maybe someday she would just give it a try.

Soon a smile broke on Julie's face, and things were back to normal once again.

The Magic of Christmas

DECEMBER 24 FELL ON the Lord's Day. In the afternoon, Allen and Julie helped deliver food baskets to needy families. Then late afternoon found Julie and Allen and the other Macintoshes on their way to the country to visit the Jacksons, friends of Macintoshes.

The two small Jackson children were excited to have visitors on Christmas Eve. They had to take Allen, Julie, Peter, and Kenny on a tour of their farm, to see their goats and calves and puppies.

It was nearly sundown when Allen and Julie stood on a flat rock looking down into the green valley below and across the misty blue hills to the fading sunset. They stood there for a long time, whispering to each other.

Soon the stars came out, one by one. Julie pointed toward the sky. "There it is!"

"Venus?" Allen looked, too. "Yes," he repeated, "there it is."

"Our Christmas star," she said.

Then, hand in hand, they walked back to the house. Inside there was a warm fire that glowed in a rustic stone fireplace. By the flickering flames, Pastor Macintosh told the Christmas story, and they all sang carols softly. Then the Macintoshes headed back to the city.

In the darkness, soft music came through the radio. There was a light chatter in the Macintosh station wagon. Allen held Julie's hand.

"Are you happy tonight, Julie?" he whispered.

"Oh, yes! Very happy. Aren't you, Allen?"

"Julie, I think I'm the happiest boy in the world! Everything's so, so perfectly wonderful. Because you're so wonderful."

Julie sighed. "That's a pretty song. What is it?"

"'Tenderly,'" he answered. "Kind of like...our friendship."

There was a brief silence.

"Everybody knows it—and accepts it now, Julie," Allen was saying.

Everybody knows what? Julie wondered.

"Yes," Allen repeated, "everybody knows—we're in love."

In love!

"I love you, Julie," he spoke gently.

And her hand tightened over his.

Back at Macintoshes, around the Christmas tree, there were presents. Without a word, Allen walked over to the tree, picked out a package tied with delicate blue ribbons, and placed it in Julie's lap.

She looked up at him. "Allen! You didn't."

He smiled. "For you. Open it."

"Now?"

He nodded.

"Open yours first," she said.

"Well—okay." He found his present from Julie, and with great gusto he tore off the paper Gloria had wrapped it in.

"A wallet!" he exclaimed. "The one *I* picked out in Mexico! Why, you wonderful little sneak!" He gave her a quick hug. "Thank you, sweetheart," he whispered.

Now it was Julie's turn. Carefully she undid the ribbon and took off the white and blue snowflake paper. Inside, she found a gold box. Her mouth flew open and she could not get the lid off fast enough. A beautiful white Bible! She looked first at the Bible, then at Allen and his family, who were all watching her. Then she picked up the Bible reverently and opened it.

"Presented to Julie Scott by Allen Macintosh, December 25, 1960. 'Study to show thyself approved unto God, a workman that needeth not to be ashamed, rightly dividing the word of truth.' II Timothy 2:15" was the inscription.

Julie was really speechless. "Oh, it's the most wonderful present I could have ever asked for! Oh, Allen! Oh!" was all she could say.

And when the others were opening their gifts, Julie and Allen were still thanking each other. Julie handled her new Bible carefully. Here on this Christmas Eve was the very essence of everything good and beautiful, everything their love stood for.

In the living room confusion of opening presents, Julie squeezed Allen's hand. "Allen, I love you, too," she said.

Christmas day dawned over Riverdale, and the Macintoshes had their Christmas dinner at Julie's house. Then they would go on a one-week vacation. This would be the first time since Allen had known Julie that they would have ever been apart for more than a day or two.

"I'll write, sweetheart," he said at the door. "Goodbye."

Julie stood by the door long after Macintoshes had left. She thought about all that had happened and wondered just what would happen from now on. She smiled as she remembered the night in November when it rained and where it had all started. She thought of the weeks since then, as they had grown to know and love each other. Now it was Christmas. *A new year was soon to begin. What would this year bring? And what about the years after that? In just three years,* she figured, *the Macintoshes would be far, far away from Riverdale since they transferred pastors to a different church every three years. But just what did the future hold?* Soon she turned from the door and got busy doing things in the house.

Allen, too, as he rode along with his family, was thinking about the wonderful Christmas Eve he had spent with Julie. Then he remembered the weekend at Pine Cove where it had all begun with Peter calling his attention to Julie. And the days after that, walking Julie home, taking teasing from Otto and Karl, and learning how to understand. *Will I ever kiss Julie? I know I want to, and I'm sure we're in love.* But he kept remembering everything his dad had told him about things like that. "A kiss is a beautiful expression of affection." But Julie was pretty special, too. He would never do anything to spoil that.

As so, soon the year closed, and the world—Julie and Allen's world—stood on the threshold of a new day. Who could imagine that a day could ever come to separate Allen and Julie with inhumane cruelty? Who dared to think that Allen and Julie would ever fight? Who could even predict the coming Valentine's Day or foresee a certain May night, a school banquet, and a white orchid? Who could know about the very next Saturday night finding them again with Gloria Martin and her boyfriend Ken Nelson? But that was the unknown, the yet-unrealized future.

New Year's Day came. Allen and Julie were in a wonderful world, real as the sunrise, romantic as springtime, but all their own and very, very special. This was young love. No one could tell when—or if—it would ever end. But it existed in the present. And it began in the November rain.

Don't miss out!

Visit the website below and you can sign up to receive emails whenever Juliana Harvard publishes a new book. There's no charge and no obligation.

https://books2read.com/r/B-A-EPQM-BYFKB

BOOKS 2 READ

Connecting independent readers to independent writers.

About the Author

Juliana Harvard's writing spans more than five decades, from her adolescence until well past midlife. It is reflective of her most emotional moments, sometimes of ecstasy and wonder, sometimes of sadness and pain, and other times of sweet melancholy and contentment beyond words.

DISCLAIMER: "These are works of fiction. Any similarities to persons and places are frequent, intentional, and occasionally brazen, but generally fragmentary, inconsistent, and disguised with fanciful invention."

–Stephen Minot, *Three Genres*